Daisy to the Rescue

For Daisy

ORCHARD BOOKS
338 Euston Road, London NW1 3BH
Orchard Books Australia
Level 17/207 Kent Street, Sydney, NSW 2000

ISBN 978 1 84616 083 7

First published in 2006 by Orchard Books
First published in paperback in 2007

Orchard Books is a division of Hachette Children's Books

Daisy to the Rescue

Jane Simmons

ORCHARD BOOKS

Daisy and Pip were playing with the chicks.
"Cheep! Cheep! Cheep!" cheeped the chicks.
But one chick went, "Quack!"
"That's Millet," said Mamma Hen.
"She wants to be a duck!"
"Coo!" said Daisy.

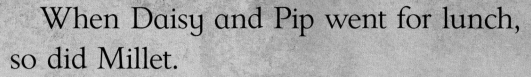

When Daisy and Pip went for lunch,
so did Millet.
"I like duck mash!" said Daisy.
"Me too!" squealed Pip.
"And me!" squeaked Millet.

And when Daisy and Pip ran in the grass,
so did Millet.

When Daisy and Pip played splash-in-the-mud,
so did Millet.

When they played peekaboo-
in-the-meadow, so did Millet.

When they played hoppity-hop on the toadstools, Daisy said, "I like hoppity-hop!"
"Me too!" squealed Pip.
"And me!" squeaked Millet.

Hoppity,

And when they reached the stream,
Daisy went splosh!
Pip went splash!
But Millet stopped at the edge.

"Wobbly twig is my favourite game!" said Daisy.
"Me too!" squealed Pip.
"Really?" trembled Millet, stepping onto the twig.

Wobble,

Wobble, wobble . . . *splosh!*

went Daisy.

Wobble, wobble . . . *splash!*

went Pip.

Daisy and Pip giggled.

Wobble,

wobble,

wobble.

But Millet didn't . . .
she clung on.

"Don't leave me behind!" cried Millet.
"Swim!" called Daisy.
"I can't swim!" cried Millet. "I'm a chicken!"
"You can't SWIM?!" yelled Daisy.

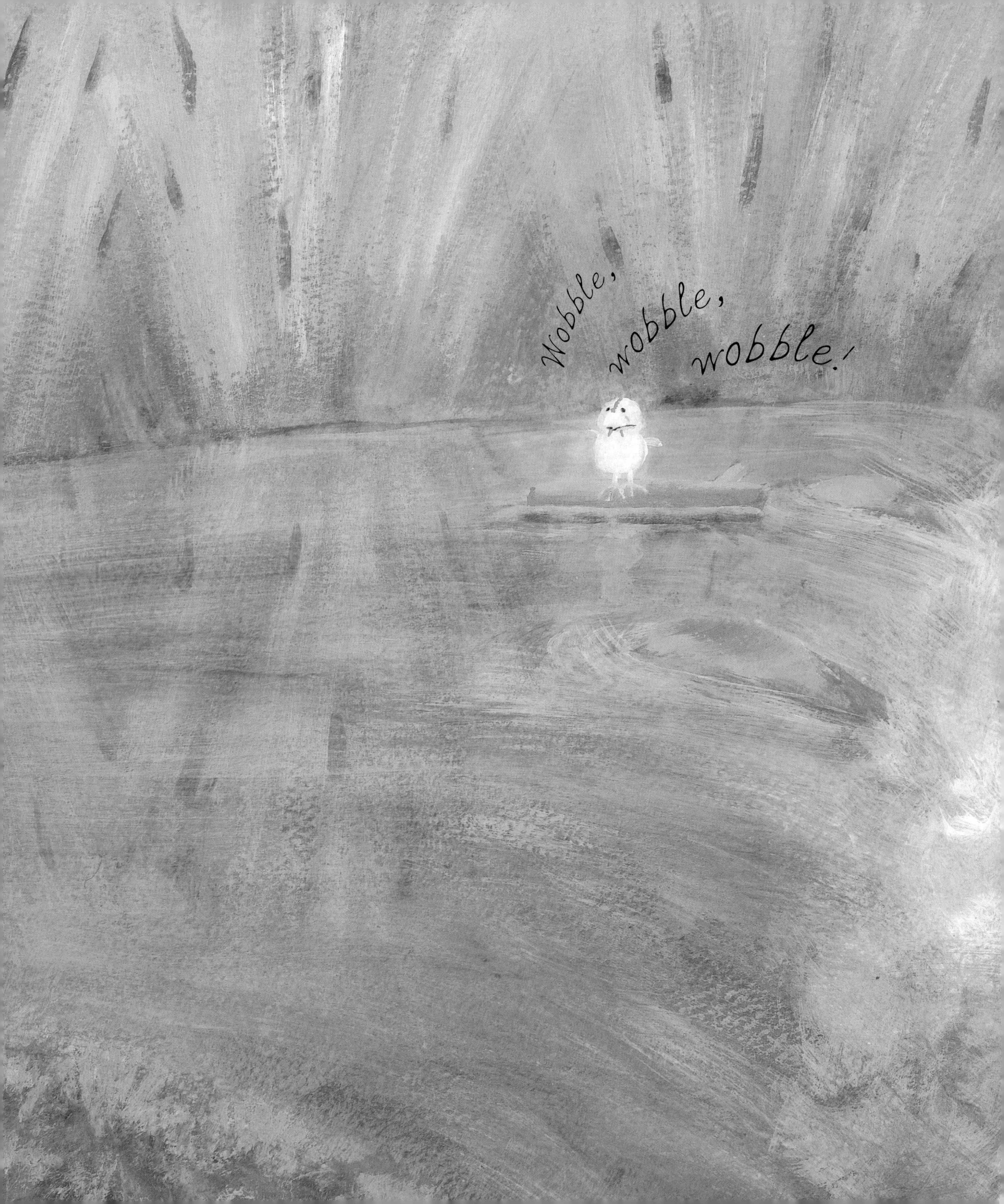

Wobble, wobble, wobble!

"Help!" cried Millet.

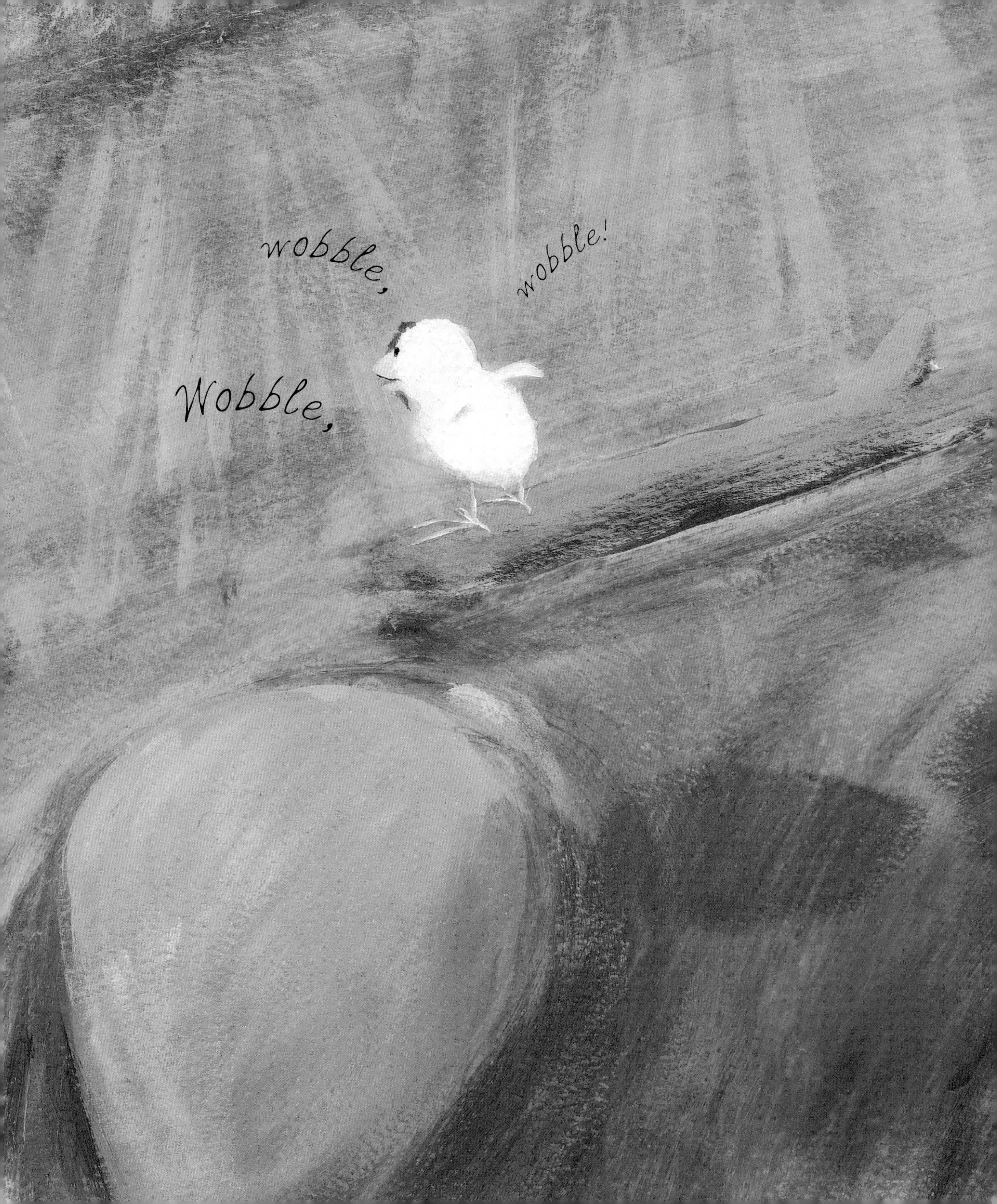

Wobble, wobble, wobble!

"Millet!"
cried everyone else.

Down and down went Millet,

and so did Daisy.

Up and up went Daisy,

and so did Millet.

"I don't like water," said Millet, unhappily.
"I'll take you to the riverbank," said Daisy.

"Oh, thank you, Daisy!" clucked Mamma Hen.
"Well done, Daisy!" said Mamma Duck.
"Cheep! Cheep! Cheep!" cheeped the chicks.

"Cheep!" went Millet.
"Coo!" said Daisy.

It was time for sleep.
"We'll play chicken games
tomorrow, Millet," said Daisy.
"My favourite!" said Millet.
"Me too!" said Pip.

And they all fell fast asleep.